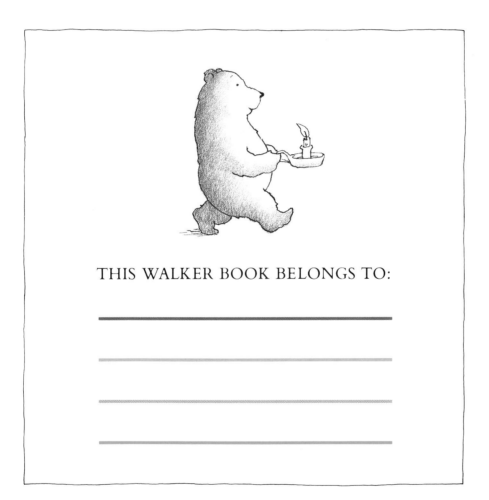

THIS WALKER BOOK BELONGS TO:

*For Charlie*
**A.B.**

---

*For Amelia*
**C.M.**

First published 1987 by
Walker Books Ltd
87 Vauxhall Walk
London SE11 5HJ

This edition published 1990

Text © 1987 Barbara Anthony
Illustrations © 1987 Claudio Munoz

Printed and bound in Italy by
L.E.G.O., Vicenza

British Library Cataloguing in Publication Data
Barber, Antonia
Satchelmouse and the dinosaurs.
Rn: Barbara Anthony  I. Title  II. Munoz, Claudio
823'.914 [J]    PZ7
ISBN 0-7445-1453-3

# Satchelmouse
### and
## THE DINOSAURS

Written by Antonia Barber

Illustrated by Claudio Muñoz

WALKER BOOKS
LONDON

The children were learning about the days when dinosaurs roamed the earth.

Mark made tree ferns from cardboard rolls and tissue paper.

Jenny made horsetail plants by cutting straws and fitting them together.

Darren was making a fierce tyrannosaurus out of papier mâché.

Sarah was trying to make a diplodocus with Plasticine, but it kept going wrong.

Sarah had a special friend, a tall brown mouse named Satchelmouse.

Inside his red jacket was a pencil case full of useful things.

The pencil sharpener was a golden trumpet and only Sarah knew that it had magic powers.

When Satchelmouse saw the diplodocus
he wrinkled up his long nose.

"It's too small," he said.

"It's a baby one," said Sarah quickly.
"They must have had babies."

"The neck should be longer."

"Maybe their necks get longer when they
are older," said Sarah hopefully.

Satchelmouse looked doubtful. "One of its legs is too short," he said.

Sarah gave up. "How can I make a diplodocus when I've never even seen one?" she said crossly.

"Never seen a diplodocus?" Satchelmouse laughed. "I can soon fix that."

He blew his golden trumpet and the magic began.

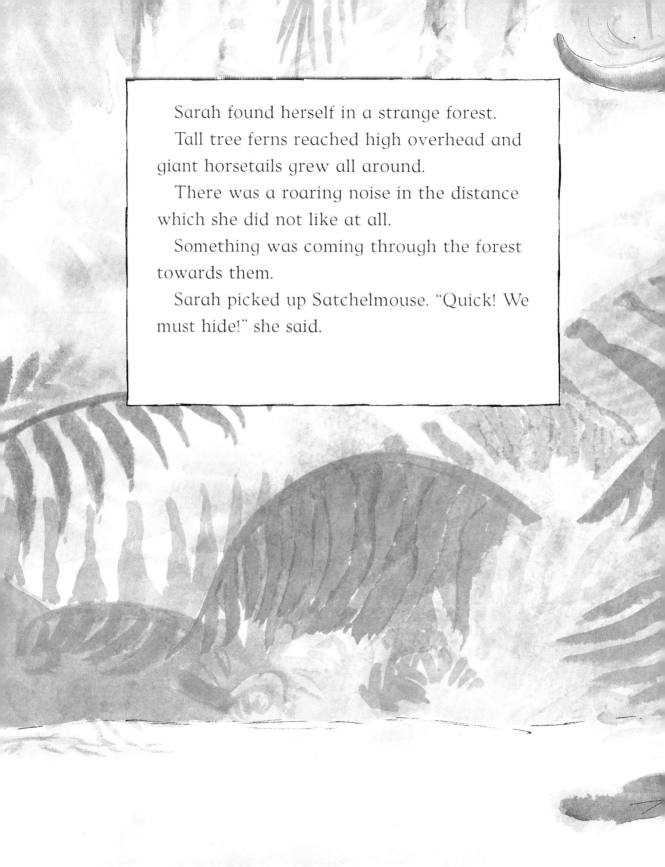

Sarah found herself in a strange forest.

Tall tree ferns reached high overhead and giant horsetails grew all around.

There was a roaring noise in the distance which she did not like at all.

Something was coming through the forest towards them.

Sarah picked up Satchelmouse. "Quick! We must hide!" she said.

They dived into a big bunch of horsetails and peered out cautiously.

It was a baby diplodocus and it was limping.

It looked around for somewhere to hide and saw Sarah's startled face.

"Help me!" it said. "The tyrannosaurus is chasing me."

The roaring noise was growing louder.

"I can't run very fast," explained the little diplodocus sadly. "One of my legs is too short."

Sarah still had some Plasticine in her hand. "I could make your leg longer if you like," she offered.

The diplodocus was very grateful. It balanced on three feet and held out the other one for Sarah to mend.

When she had finished, it frisked about
with little cries of joy.

Sarah was afraid that the tyrannosaurus
would hear it.

"Haven't you got a mother to look after
you?" she asked.

"I've lost her." The little diplodocus
looked sad again. "If only my neck was
longer I could look over the treetops
and find her."

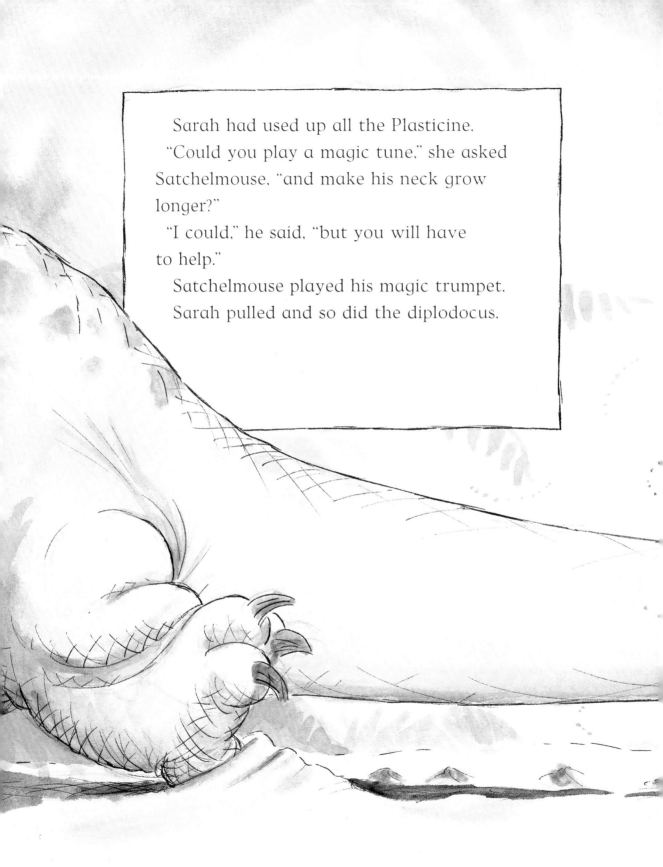

Sarah had used up all the Plasticine.

"Could you play a magic tune," she asked Satchelmouse, "and make his neck grow longer?"

"I could," he said, "but you will have to help."

Satchelmouse played his magic trumpet.

Sarah pulled and so did the diplodocus.

Soon its neck was so long that it could look over the tops of the tree ferns.

"Oh, thank you!" said the little diplodocus. "I can see my mother now!" And it went bounding off towards her through the forest.

The roaring noise was very close.

"Quick! Blow your trumpet!" said Sarah to Satchelmouse. "I want to go back to school."

But the tyrannosaurus had already found them.

Sarah saw its big white teeth gleaming as it opened its mouth to gobble her up.

"Help!" she shouted. But Satchelmouse was hiding under some ferns.

Sarah thought she heard the faintest trumpet squeak.

Suddenly all the big white teeth vanished. The fierce tyrannosaurus did not have a single tooth in its head!

Sarah found that she was back in the classroom.

Satchelmouse was under her chair.

As Sarah picked him up she heard Darren say, "Stupid tyrannosaurus! His teeth have fallen out."

Mrs James liked the diplodocus. "It looks very real," she said.

Sarah laughed and picked up a big lump of Plasticine.

"I'm going to make him a mother now," she said.